PUFFIN BOOKS

Unicorn School

The Treasure Hunt

At last all the teams had their maps and
bags and were ready to start.
The Tricorn raised his head so that his
horn sparkled in the sunlight. 'Let the
treasure hunt begin!'

Linda Chapman lives in Leicestershire with her family and two Bernese mountain dogs. She used to be a stage manager in the theatre. When she is not writing she spends her time looking after her two young daughters, horse riding and teaching drama. You can find out more about Linda on her website lindachapman.co.uk or visit mysecretunicorn.co.uk.

Books by Linda Chapman

BRIGHT LIGHTS
CENTRE STAGE

MY SECRET UNICORN series

NOT QUITE A MERMAID series

STARDUST series

UNICORN SCHOOL series
(*Titles in reading order*)
FIRST CLASS FRIENDS
THE SURPRISE PARTY
THE TREASURE HUNT

Unicorn School

The Treasure Hunt

Linda Chapman

Illustrated by Ann Kronheimer

PUFFIN

PUFFIN BOOKS

Published by the Penguin Group
Penguin Books Ltd, 80 Strand, London WC2R ORL, England
Penguin Group (USA) Inc., 375 Hudson Street, New York, New York 10014, USA
Penguin Group (Canada), 90 Eglinton Avenue East, Suite 700, Toronto, Ontario, Canada M4P 2Y3
(a division of Pearson Penguin Canada Inc.)
Penguin Ireland, 25 St Stephen's Green, Dublin 2, Ireland (a division of Penguin Books Ltd)
Penguin Group (Australia), 250 Camberwell Road, Camberwell, Victoria 3124, Australia
(a division of Pearson Australia Group Pty Ltd)
Penguin Books India Pvt Ltd, 11 Community Centre, Panchsheel Park,
New Delhi – 110 017, India
Penguin Group (NZ), 67 Apollo Drive, Rosedale, North Shore 0632, New Zealand
(a division of Pearson New Zealand Ltd)
Penguin Books (South Africa) (Pty) Ltd, 24 Sturdee Avenue, Rosebank,
Johannesburg 2196, South Africa

Penguin Books Ltd, Registered Offices: 80 Strand, London WC2R ORL, England

puffinbooks.com

First published 2008
1

Set in Bembo
Typeset by Palimpsest Book Production Limited, Grangemouth, Stirlingshire
Made and printed in England by Clays Ltd, St Ives plc

British Library Cataloguing in Publication Data
A CIP catalogue record for this book is available from the British Library

ISBN: 978-0-141-32249-0

To Luca Misra, who is a real treasure

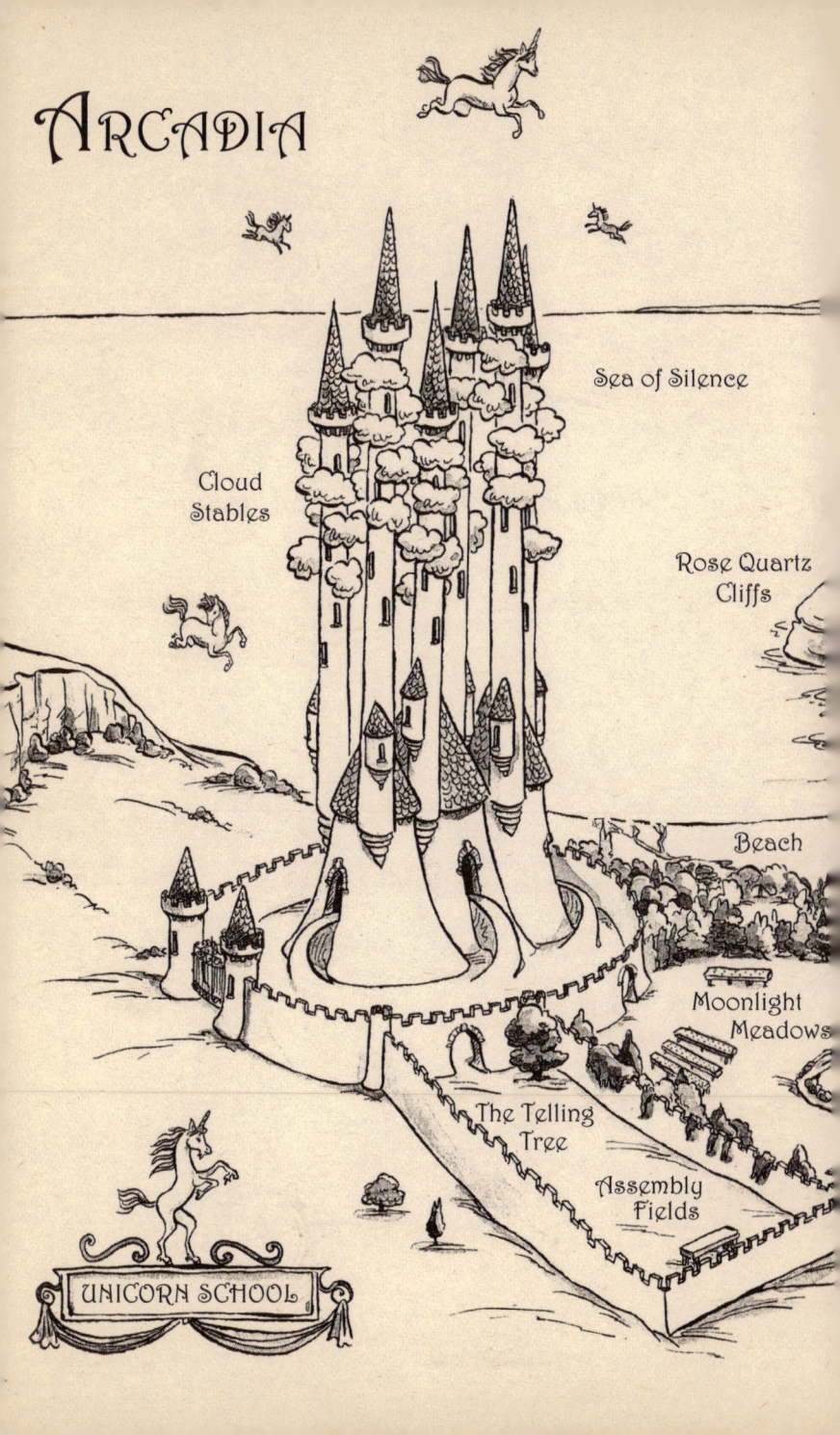

ARCADIA

Sea of Silence

Cloud
Stables

Rose Quartz
Cliffs

Beach

Moonlight
Meadows

The Telling
Tree

Assembly
Fields

UNICORN SCHOOL

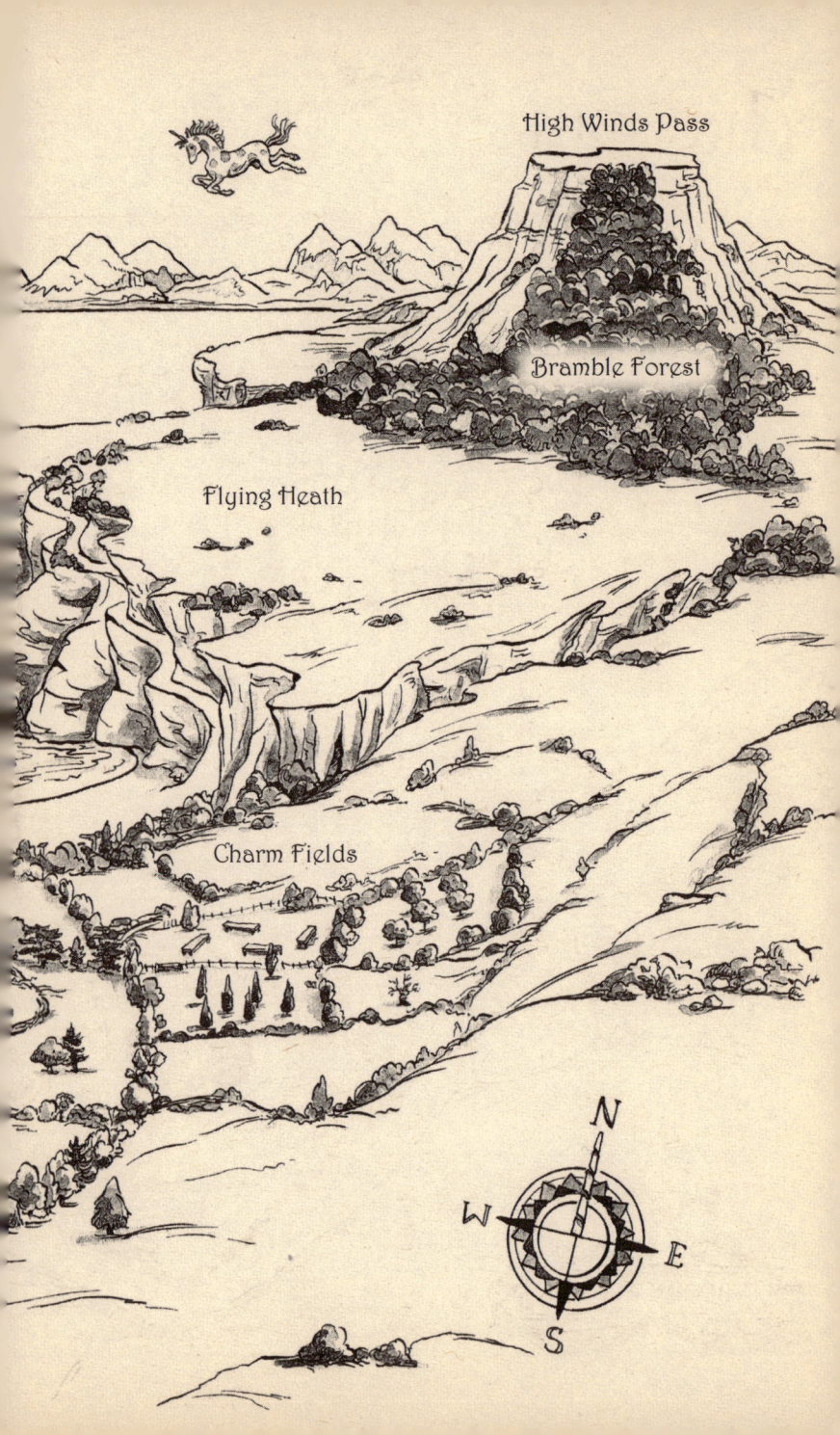

High Winds Pass

Bramble Forest

Flying Heath

Charm Fields

N
W   E
S

Contents

Chapter One

Exciting News!

'Oh, wow!' Willow stared at the new poster pinned on to the school notice board. The title was written in large purple letters:

WINTER TREASURE HUNT!

Willow read quickly:

A treasure hunt will take place this Saturday, starting at 10 a.m. All unicorns in the school may take part but they must be in teams of four. The clues will be hidden around Arcadia by the teachers. Each team will have six clues to solve that will lead them to six objects. The first team back with all their objects will win a term's supply of shamrock! All teams wishing to take part must register with the chief elf by Friday.

Willow snorted in excitement. A treasure hunt! She couldn't wait to tell her best friends, Sapphire, Storm and Troy. She was sure they would want to enter. *We can be a team together*, she thought. *It'll be such fun!*

She set off across the Assembly Fields towards Moonlight Meadows where she had last seen her friends.

Willow and her friends were all in Year One at Unicorn School. All the unicorns who lived in Arcadia went to school when they were nine to learn how to use their magic powers. They stayed at school until they were fifteen and when they left, the cleverest and bravest unicorns were chosen to be the Guardians of Arcadia. It was the job of the Guardians to look after all the other creatures who lived there. Willow loved being at Unicorn

School and she really hoped she would be a Guardian one day!

She cantered into Moonlight Meadows where all the unicorns ate and where they usually hung out between classes. The elves who worked at the school were clearing away lunch from four long tables. There were unicorns chatting, playing tag, grazing by the stream, flying through the air. Willow spotted her three friends near one of the oak trees.

'Hi, Willow!' said Sapphire as Willow cantered over. 'Where have you been?'

'Looking at the school notice board. You'll never guess what!' Willow exclaimed.

'What?' Troy asked curiously. He was a very sporty-looking unicorn with a noble face and long golden horn.

'There's going to be a treasure hunt!' Willow's eyes sparkled. 'Isn't that cool? It's on Saturday, for teams of four.'

'We can be a team!' said Storm. He was very big for his age but was very gentle and kind. 'We can all go in it together.'

'I've heard about the school having treasure hunts,' said Troy. 'They organize them to help us learn about the different bits of Arcadia.'

'Did the notice say what the prize is?' Storm asked Willow.

'A term's supply of shamrock!' Willow declared.

Her friends all whinnied excitedly. Shamrock was their favourite food.

It had magic in its leaves and tasted sweet and tingly.

'I hope we win!' said Storm.

'Me too, but even if we don't, it should be great just taking part,' Sapphire put in.

Storm and Willow nodded but Troy shook his head. 'I don't want just to take part, I want to win!'

Willow grinned at him. 'You always want to win everything, Troy!'

'That's because winning's fun,' said Troy. 'We'd better get practising.'

'Practising?' Storm echoed.

'How *can* you practise for a treasure hunt?' Sapphire asked in surprise.

'Well, we can practise flying and galloping as fast as we can,' said Troy. 'And we can study old treasure hunt maps and practise solving the clues on them. And learn the maps of Arcadia. There's loads of stuff we can do.'

It all sounded a lot of work to Willow.

Just then one of the elves blew a note on a large shell.

'We'd better go,' Sapphire said. 'Or we'll be late for class.'

Willow followed the others across the meadows, excitement buzzing through her. This treasure hunt was going to be fun!

The Healing Lesson

'Good afternoon, class,' Sirona, the healing teacher, said as all the Year One unicorns gathered round her at the start of the lesson. 'Today I am going to tell you about some of the magical creatures in Arcadia that you may one day need to heal if you become a Guardian, and then we will practise your own healing skills using some plants.'

Healing was one of Willow's favourite subjects at school. But as Sirona talked about the different magical creatures that lived in Arcadia, Willow found herself daydreaming about the treasure hunt. How many other teams would enter? How difficult would the clues be? Whereabouts in Arcadia would they be sent? Willow hadn't been to many places in Arcadia. She only really knew the meadows and woods where her parents lived and the school grounds. It would be so much fun to go exploring!

Suddenly she was aware that

Sirona had just asked the class a question about kelpies – a type of pixie-like creature that lived in streams.

I'd better concentrate, Willow thought guiltily as she realized she couldn't answer the question because she hadn't been listening to what Sirona was saying.

But it was hard when the thoughts of the treasure hunt were whirling around in her brain and Willow was glad when Sirona stopped talking and they actually got to do some healing magic themselves.

Sirona gave them each a wilted plant. The flower head and leaves on each plant were all floppy.

'I would like you to try to heal
the plant I have given you,' Sirona
said. 'Concentrate on feeling well
and healthy. Let that feeling grow in
your mind and then touch the plant
with your horn. Your horn will start
to glow if the magic is working. If
your magic is strong enough the
plant will be healed.'

Willow looked at her plant. Its orange flower was drooping sadly. *I can do this*, she thought confidently. She was good at healing. She shut her eyes and thought about feeling healthy. She let the feeling build and grow and when it felt as if it was about to burst out of her, she opened her eyes and touched her horn to the orange flower. Sparks seemed to shoot through her. Her horn glowed a brilliant silver and she felt magic flowing from her into the flower. To her delight, the flower began to move upwards towards the sky and the stalk stiffened. Willow took her horn away. The flower was healed!

'Well done, Willow!' Sirona exclaimed.

Willow looked around the class. Although some of the others had managed to make their flowers look a bit healthier, no one else had managed to heal their plant the way she had. Sirona smiled. 'You have a natural talent for healing, Willow. Maybe you'll be a Guardian of Arcadia one day.'

Willow glowed. Sirona couldn't have said anything to make her happier. 'I'd love to be!' she said.

After the class had finished, Storm, Sapphire and Troy joined Willow as they headed back to Moonlight Meadows.

'You healed your plant really well,' Storm said to Willow.

'Thanks.' Willow smiled.

'I wish I was as good as you,' said Sapphire enviously. 'I'm useless at healing. My plant didn't get better at all.'

'You're loads better than me at rose-quartz gazing, though,' Willow told her. 'You always manage to see things in the rose quartz. I usually just get a blur.'

When unicorns touched their horns to rocks of rose quartz they were supposed to be able to use their magic to try and see what was happening in other parts of Arcadia. But it was quite tricky to do.

'We're all good at different things,' said Storm. 'I really liked it when Sirona was telling us about the other magical creatures in Arcadia. I never knew that dragons sometimes lose their puff, or that kelpies can catch colds.'

Sapphire nodded. 'It was really interesting.'

Willow began to wish she'd listened harder at the beginning of the lesson. 'What was Sirona saying?' she asked.

Troy snorted. 'How can you three talk about boring lessons when we've got the treasure hunt to think about? After tea tonight let's go to the library and look up old treasure hunt maps and practise solving the clues. Then tomorrow morning why don't we meet early and practise flying?'

Willow exchanged looks with the other two.

'Do we really need to?' Storm asked.

'Yes,' Troy said bossily. 'We do.

We'll meet at the library at six o'clock. OK?'

They nodded slowly. 'OK,' they all said.

Troy stamped his hoof. 'When we win the treasure hunt you'll thank me. Just wait and see!'

Troy, Willow, Storm and Sapphire met at the library at six o'clock as planned.

'The maps and clues for the old treasure hunts are kept over here,' Troy whispered, leading the way to the back of the big room. 'I spoke to the librarian earlier and she said it was fine for us to look at them. The clues will all be different on this year's hunt so it's not cheating, it's just practising.'

He pulled a dark leather book off the shelf with his mouth and put it down on a nearby table. They all crowded round. Inside there were ten maps of Arcadia, each with six clues to different places and a set of answers.

'Look at all these names,' Willow said. There were so many places marked on the map. She read some of them out: 'Dragon's Peak, Mermaid Beach, Butterfly Hollow, Cockatrice Cavern, Lion Forest, Echo Cove, Phoenix Mountain.' She looked at the others. 'Oh, wow, I can't *wait* to go exploring!'

'Let's read the clues and see if we can work out where they are leading to,' Troy said. 'Here's the first one. It's supposed to help you find a place on the map.' He read out: '"*I have a floor but no walls or a door. I make no noise but I sound like I roar.*"'

Sapphire looked blank. 'What does that mean?'

'I don't know,' said Willow. 'What's got a floor but no walls or a door?'

'A forest!' said Storm. 'It's an easy clue. I bet it means go to Lion Forest. A forest has a floor but no walls or a door and it doesn't make any noise but its name makes it sound as if it roars.'

'You're right!' said Troy, checking the answers.

'Let's try another one,' said Willow. She read out: "*Scales aplenty and snorting flame, follow me to play the game.*"

Once again Storm got the answer really quickly. 'I think it means go to Dragon's Peak because dragons breathe fire and have scales.'

Sapphire checked the list of answers. 'You're right again. You're really good at this, Storm.'

'I like solving problems,' Storm said happily.

'This is brilliant!' said Troy, looking delighted. 'We'll stand a great chance of winning with you answering all the clues, Storm.'

They practised solving more clues and then Troy spread all the maps out on the table. 'Now, let's try and memorize these,' he said. 'They've all got different bits of Arcadia labelled on them. If we learn them all, we'll know where all the places are and when we get our clues on Saturday we won't have to spend ages

looking over the map trying to
decide how to get there.'

'Do we have to? I'm tired now,'
Willow said.

'Me too,' Sapphire yawned.

Storm nodded. 'We can look at
the maps tomorrow, Troy.'

'I want to look now!' Troy insisted.

Storm and Sapphire hesitated but
Willow shook her head firmly.
'Count me out. I think it's silly. We
don't need to learn the maps. We'll
have a map with us.'

'Fine,' Troy said huffily. 'You lot go
back to the stables then but I'm
going to stay and learn the maps
because I think it'll help us to win.'

Sapphire, Storm and Willow left

him in the library. 'Troy's taking this treasure hunt really seriously, isn't he?' said Sapphire.

Willow nodded. 'I wish he could see that it's going to be fun whether we win or not.'

'Do you think he *will* try and make us get up early to practise flying?' Storm said.

'I hope not,' said Sapphire. She didn't like getting up early.

Willow grinned. 'I bet he will!'

Chapter
Three

Flying Through Snow!

'Wakey wakey!'
Willow blinked her eyes open the next morning. Troy was standing next to her in the stall. He poked her with his horn. 'Come on! We're going to practise flying, Willow!' He bounced out of her stall. 'Time to wake up,

Sapphire! Come on, Storm!'

Willow yawned and got slowly to her feet. It was *very* early in the morning.

'Do we *have* to get up now?' she heard Sapphire complain.

'Yes!' Troy said. 'The more practice we get the better and it's a lovely morning for flying!'

They all left the cloud stable and went outside. Troy was certainly right about it being a lovely morning. The sun was shining although it was very cold. The grass in Moonlight Meadows was covered with frost and their breath froze on the air.

'Come on, come on!' Troy said

bossily as soon as they reached the Flying Heath. 'Line up and let's practise racing starts.'

'But why?' Willow asked. 'We're not going in for a race, we're going on a treasure hunt!'

'Yes, but every second might count,' said Troy.

Willow opened her mouth to argue but Sapphire nudged her. 'Just do what he says,' she said in a low voice. 'Otherwise we'll never get back in time for breakfast!'

Willow knew Sapphire was right so she didn't say anything but lined up with the others.

'On your marks. Get set. Go!' Troy shouted.

They all took off. Troy was easily the quickest but he always was. He was one of the fastest unicorns in the whole school even though he was only a Year One.

'Come on, you can do better than that!' he said to the rest of them. 'Try again! Storm, you have to push off quicker – push down with both of your back legs. Sapphire, you took off OK but then you slowed down – you must keep going. And Willow, you didn't look as if you were trying at all. Let's have another go.'

They lined up again. Storm looked flustered. He tried too hard to push off with his back legs and ended up shooting straight into the air and losing control. Sapphire was concentrating so hard on trying to keep flying fast after she'd taken off that she didn't see him.

'Ow!' they both gasped as they banged into each other. They weren't hurt and they both started to laugh.

Willow giggled too and landed. 'I don't think your training's doing us much good,' she said teasingly to Troy.

He glared at her and then at the others. 'You're not taking this seriously enough. Now come on. Let's try again!'

Willow was very relieved when the horn blew for breakfast time. 'I'm glad the treasure hunt's tomorrow,' she muttered to Sapphire. 'Imagine if it was weeks away and Troy made us do this *every* morning.'

Sapphire shuddered at the thought. 'He is being a bit annoying.'

'A bit?' said Willow. 'A lot! I wish he didn't want to win so much.'

They trotted thankfully to the table. There were buckets full of a warm bran mash mixed up with carrots and apples all along the table.

'Yum!' said Willow, plunging her head into a bucket. It was her favourite breakfast on a cold day!

As she finished the last mouthful she felt something soft and cold land on her head. She looked up. 'Snow!' she gasped as she saw flakes of snow floating down from the sky. 'It's snowing!'

The other unicorns whinnied in excitement.

'Oh, wow!' said Troy. 'We'll get to fly through it in our flying lesson after breakfast.'

'And at lunchtime we can make a snow unicorn,' said Sapphire. 'I hope it falls really thickly!'

★

After breakfast, they headed off to the Flying Heath for their first lesson of the day. Atlas, their flying teacher, was waiting for them. 'We were going to practise turning and changing direction today,' he told them. 'But I think we'll practise flying through snow instead. Has anyone used their magic to fly through snow before?'

The Year Ones all shook their heads. Unicorns didn't usually do much magic before they started school and it was the first time it had snowed since they had begun there.

'Well, I think you're really going to enjoy it,' Atlas told them.

Storm raised his horn. 'Isn't it a bit hard to fly through snow?'

'Yes,' put in Flint, another Year One unicorn. 'It must be really hard to see.'

'It would be but we have a special type of magic we can use to help us,' said Atlas. 'To make it work, you must imagine feeling as warm as you can. Let the feeling flow out through your horn and see what happens. Off you go!'

The unicorns rose into the sky.

Feel warm, feel warm, Willow thought to herself. She imagined feeling toasty and snug in her cloud stall. The sensation rose inside her but then the next minute she found

herself swerving out of control and
heading straight towards the ground.
She whizzed upwards just in time. It
was really hard to concentrate on
flying and to think about feeling
warm at the same time!

Looking round she was relieved to
see that she wasn't the only one
having difficulty doing both. All
around her, unicorns were swerving
and crashing into each other. But
then she caught her breath. High
above them all, Troy was flying
through the snow. Purple stars
streamed from the tip of his horn.
They flowed together into an arch
over his back, casting a glow all
around him. As the snowflakes fell

on the arch they melted. Troy flew
through the snow in a bubble of
magic lilac light.

Willow caught her breath and for
a moment forgot how annoyed she
was with Troy for being so bossy
about the treasure hunt. He really
was brilliant at anything to do with

flying. 'Well done!' she shouted, cantering up into the air.

He grinned at her as she joined him. 'Thanks, Willow! This is cool!'

'I can't do it at all,' said Willow, shaking her head as the flakes blinded her. 'I'm going to have to go back down.'

'No, wait,' said Troy. 'Here, fly with me under my light and then see if you can make the magic work too.'

'OK,' said Willow eagerly. She reached his side and, cantering along in time with him through the air, she found that his magic light kept the snowflakes off her as well.

She tried to imagine a feeling of warmth again. But as she

concentrated on it she felt herself starting to worry that she was going to crash, so she quickly stopped.

'Don't worry,' Troy told her, nudging her neck with his nose. 'I'll make sure you don't fly into anything. Try again.'

Willow flew even closer to him so their sides were touching and then concentrated again. This time the feeling of warmth flooded through her and out of her horn. Suddenly, purple stars of her own started to appear. 'I'm doing it!' she gasped as a rainbow of light formed over her body.

'You *are* doing it!' exclaimed Troy. 'Now you can concentrate on flying

too.' He edged away. 'See, you're on
your own!'

Willow realized she was. She
whinnied in delight. Together they
cantered and swooped through the
snowy sky.

'Well done!' Atlas cried, coming
over to them. 'It normally takes a
lot of practice to be able to fly
through snow.'

'It was Troy!' said Willow gratefully. 'He helped me. I couldn't have done it without him!'

Troy looked very pleased. 'You did it yourself, really, I just gave you a bit of help.'

'Well, it's really great to see you both working as a team,' said Atlas. 'Off you go!'

Willow and Troy flew into the sky. 'Now you know how to do it, let's go and help the others,' said Troy, looking over to where Storm and Sapphire were trying to fly through the snow but failing. 'I'll help Storm learn, you can help Sapphire.'

'OK,' said Willow, thrilled with her new skill. 'Come on!'

Chapter
Four

Troy's Treasure
Hunters

By the end of the flying lesson, Sapphire and Storm were swooping and diving through the snow as easily as Willow and Troy. It was lovely just to be having fun together rather than to be arguing about the treasure hunt, but the peace didn't last for long. At lunchtime, Troy remembered they had to practise and tried to get them all to go to the library to look at the maps again.

'But I want to make a snow unicorn,' said Storm. 'We don't know how long the snow will last.'

'Yeah,' agreed Willow. 'We can look at boring maps another time!'

'The treasure hunt's tomorrow,' Troy told them. 'We should use all the time we have and we also need to think of a name to give our team. We have to register it by the end of today.'

Sapphire sighed. 'OK, let's go to the library then and do some treasure hunt stuff.'

But Willow shook her head. She didn't want to spend all lunchtime in the library. 'No, I'm not going,' she decided. 'I'm going to make a snow unicorn!'

'Willow!' Troy said crossly. 'Don't you care about this treasure hunt at all?'

'Of course I do. I just don't see why we need to waste our time learning maps,' Willow argued. 'It won't help!'

'Yes it will! You're being stupid!' Troy told her.

'And you're just being annoying!' she snapped angrily.

'Stop it, you two!' Sapphire broke in.

Willow and Troy shut up.

'Don't argue,' said Sapphire, stepping forward. 'Please!'

Troy looked at her. 'You'll come and learn the maps with me, won't you, Sapphire?' he said pleadingly.

'Well . . .' Sapphire looked torn. 'Oh, OK, then,' she sighed.

'Storm, you'll come and make a snow unicorn with me, won't you?' Willow said quickly.

Storm looked unhappy. 'Can't we

do something all together?' he said.

But Troy was already trotting away with a reluctant Sapphire.

'It looks like we can't,' Willow told Storm. 'Or at least not while Troy's being so crazy about winning this treasure hunt. Oh well.' She tried to be cheerful. 'I bet we'll have a much better time than they will!'

But it wasn't nearly as much fun making a snow unicorn on their own.

'There!' Willow said brightly, stepping back after a while. 'It looks great.'

Storm looked at it. 'I suppose . . . but we'd have been able to make a

much bigger one if Troy and
Sapphire had helped us. And it *would*
have been more fun. It's always
better when we do things together
– like when you and Troy helped
Sapphire and me learn to fly
through snow earlier. That was
brilliant.'

Willow sighed. She was still feeling
cross with Troy but she knew Storm
was right. It *was* more fun when
they did things together.

Just then Sapphire came back.
'Hey! That looks great!' she said,
looking at their snow unicorn. 'Can
I help finish it off?'

'Of course,' Willow told her.
'Where's Troy?'

'I don't know. He said he had to do something for the treasure hunt and went off.' Sapphire looked at the snow unicorn. 'I wish we could have helped you make the unicorn. I like it much more when we do stuff all together,' she said wistfully.

'So you didn't have loads of fun in the library, then?' Willow asked.

'No.' Sapphire looked guilty and giggled. 'Don't tell Troy this but it was really boring!'

Storm nuzzled her. 'Well, we missed you. Come on, let's finish this snow unicorn.'

They were just finishing off by putting stones in for the snow unicorn's eyes when Troy came cantering into the meadows. Willow noticed he was looking very pleased with himself. 'All done!' he announced.

'What's all done?' Willow asked curiously.

'I've registered our team for the treasure hunt,' said Troy.

'You've registered us,' said Storm

in surprise. 'But that means you must have chosen a name.'

Troy shook his mane back. 'Yep! I've called us . . .' he paused, looking very proud, 'Troy's Treasure Hunters!'

They all stared at him.

'Troy's Treasure Hunters!' Willow echoed.

Troy nodded. 'It's a cool name, isn't it?'

'Um . . .' Sapphire began slowly.

'No!' Willow broke in. 'It's not a cool name at all! It makes us sound like we're your team! You shouldn't have registered without talking to the rest of us, Troy!'

'Well, none of the rest of you seemed that interested in this treasure hunt.' Troy looked cross. 'I think you should be grateful to me.'

'We are,' Sapphire said hastily. 'It's fine, Troy. Thank you for registering us.'

Troy stamped huffily. 'I'll see you later!' He cantered off.

Willow swung round to the others. 'I can't believe he registered the team's name without talking to us about it!'

'I wish he hadn't,' said Storm. 'But he didn't mean to upset us, Willow.'

'No, I'm sure he didn't,' said Sapphire.

'Huh,' Willow snorted. She looked in the direction Troy had gone. 'I'm going to be glad when the treasure hunt's over. I almost wish it wasn't happening!'

Sapphire nuzzled her. 'Don't be like that. You know it will be fun. Troy's just being his usual bossy self. Try to ignore him and just have a good time. That's what I'm going to do.'

Willow looked at her and felt a rush of affection. Sapphire was so sensible. And she was right. There really was no point getting upset about Troy wanting to win so much and being so bossy. That was just the way he was. 'OK,' she said, nuzzling Sapphire back. 'It'll still be fun even if Troy is being the biggest bossyboots ever.' She took a deep breath. 'I promise I'll try really hard not to get cross with him tomorrow. I'll just enjoy myself!'

Sapphire whinnied. 'Cool!'

Storm nodded. 'We're all going to have a great time. I know we are!'

Chapter Five

The Treasure Hunt

When Willow woke up the
following day she looked out
of the window. More snow had
fallen in the night and the sun was
shining in a clear blue sky.
Excitement fizzed through her. It
was the day of the treasure hunt and
even the thought of Troy being

bossy all day couldn't dampen her happiness.

She could hear the others around her all getting up. The other unicorns who shared their stable – Topaz, Starlight, Flint and Ash – were also going in for the treasure hunt as a team.

'See you down there,' Topaz called to Willow as Willow left the stable.

'Yeah, good luck today,' Willow told her.

Topaz smiled. 'You too!'

'What are you doing wishing the other team good luck, Willow?' Troy told her crossly as he joined her on the way to breakfast.

Willow felt a flicker of annoyance

but she squashed it down. 'I was just trying to be friendly,' she replied.

Troy opened his mouth but Willow trotted away before he could say anything else that would annoy her. 'Come on. I'm hungry!'

They all ate their breakfast as fast as they could. Everyone was talking about the treasure hunt. Nearly everyone in the school was going to be taking part.

'I had another look at the maps yesterday evening,' Troy hissed to Willow, Sapphire and Storm. 'I think I know them off by heart now. I should be able to find the way to any of the places we have to go to.'

'Wouldn't it be amazing if we won the shamrock?' Sapphire said.

'A whole term's supply!' said Storm. 'Where are the teachers keeping it?'

'In one of the feed rooms near the kitchens,' said Troy, who seemed to know everything there was to know about the treasure hunt. 'One of the elves told me that shamrock mustn't get too cold or it goes off and can't be eaten. They're going to bring it out at the start of the treasure hunt in boxes.' He looked around. 'Let's go to the Assembly Fields as soon as we've finished breakfast. That's where the teachers will be giving out the maps. Maybe we can get ours early and start working out what the first clue means!'

But although Willow's team was one of the first teams into the Assembly Fields, Atlas wouldn't let them have their treasure map. 'No one is going to have their map until the treasure hunt officially starts,' the flying teacher told them. 'The Tricorn is going to talk to all those taking part and then we'll give out the maps so that everyone gets them at the same time.'

By a quarter to ten, the Assembly Fields were full of excited unicorns standing in teams of four. They all fell silent as the Tricorn – the school's Headmaster – walked into the field. He was a very noble-looking unicorn with a horn of three colours – bronze, silver and gold – and he was accompanied by a team of elves all carrying wooden boxes that they placed in front of the platform.

The Tricorn walked on to the platform and looked around at the expectant unicorns. As the last box was put down, he began to speak. 'Good morning, everyone. I'm glad to see so many of you taking part in the annual winter treasure hunt this year. As you know, you have to try and find six objects. This year, they will be six crystals all labelled with your team's name. To find the crystals you must follow the clues. The first team back with all six of their crystals will win the prize.' He nodded towards the wooden crates and smiled. 'A term's supply of shamrock. Fly swiftly, solve your clues wisely and the prize might be yours. Only one team can win but I hope that you will all gain something from visiting the different places in Arcadia as you collect your objects. Good luck, teams! The teachers will now give out the treasure maps. Please do not turn them over until the chief elf blows his horn.'

The teachers trotted among the teams giving out the maps. They also gave each team a leather bag to put their crystals into.

'I'll wear it,' said Troy quickly. He took the bag from Atlas and slipped it over his head.

Willow frowned but she was still determined she wasn't going to get cross with Troy. She didn't want *anything* to ruin the day.

At last all the teams had their maps and bags and were ready to start.

The Tricorn raised his head so that his horn sparkled in the sunlight. 'Let the treasure hunt begin!'

The chief elf blew a long note and all the teams turned their maps over. Willow noticed that not all the bits of Arcadia were named, just some of them.

'What does the first clue say?' Storm asked eagerly.

The clue to the first place they had to go to was written at the top of the map.

'Clue one,' Troy read out. '"*A very pretty thing am I, you'll see me in the pale-blue sky. Delicate, fragile on the wing, indeed I am a pretty thing. What am I?*"'

They all looked at each other.

Willow re-read the clue. 'A pretty thing? On the wing? What does it mean?'

'We've got to be quick!' Troy urged, glancing round. 'Some of the other teams are setting off already.'

'Maybe it's talking about a bird,' Sapphire suggested. 'Look, there is a place on the map called Bird's View. It could mean we have to go there.'

'Great! Let's go!' said Troy, taking off.

'No, Troy! Wait!' exclaimed Storm. 'It's not a bird. A bird's a good guess, Sapphire, but they're not really delicate and fragile, are they? I think it's a butterfly!'

'Which means we probably need to go to Butterfly Hollow!' said Willow. 'I bet you're right, Storm.'

'I know how to get there,' said Troy. 'Come on!'

They took off after him. They flew above the Assembly Fields and out across the courtyard. The air was filled with unicorns all flying in different directions as they followed their clues.

'Wait, Troy!' Willow called as Troy raced ahead.

'We can't keep up!' Sapphire whinnied to him.

But Troy didn't stop.

'Troy!' shouted Willow as she galloped through the sky. 'We don't know the way to Butterfly Hollow.' But he was too far off to hear. He flew into the distance.

'It's OK. I've still got the map,' said Storm. 'Let's land and have a look at it and see if we can work out where to go.'

'Troy should have waited!' said Willow as they landed and Storm shook out the map. 'He knows we can't fly as fast as him!'

'Don't worry. It's not too far away,' said Sapphire. 'Look, we just have to fly over that line of trees and we'll be there.'

They raced into the sky again. They were all out of breath when they finally reached Butterfly Hollow.

Troy was standing on a grassy hill, surrounded by white and yellow butterflies. He had a bright blue crystal with a piece of paper attached to it in his mouth. 'What took you so long?' he exclaimed, dropping the crystal on to the grass.

'You know we can't fly as fast as you!' Willow said. 'You should have waited, Troy. We didn't know where we were going so we had to look at the map. What's the point of you knowing all the places if you fly off so we still have to keep looking at the map to find where you've gone?'

Troy looked taken aback. 'Oh.' It was obvious he hadn't thought about that. 'I guess I should have waited. Sorry.' He looked at the crystal at his hooves and pricked his ears. 'Well, at least you're here now and I've found the second clue so we can get on and solve it. Listen. "*You heard me before and yet hear me again. Then I go until you call me again*",' he read out. 'It's a really tricky one.'

'No, it isn't!' said Storm. 'The answer to the clue is an echo! You hear echoes again and again and then they go away until you make another noise, or, as the clue says, "call me again". Look,' he put the map down and pointed with his horn. 'There's a place called Echo Cove. I bet that's where we have to go!'

'Cool!' exclaimed Troy. 'Let's go!'

'Wait!' called Willow. But even though Troy did slow down and wait for them this time, he couldn't resist speeding up as they drew near to Echo Cove – a small sandy beach by the sea.

By the time the other three had landed, Troy had already discovered their next clue. It was attached to an emerald-green crystal that he had found half buried in the sand. 'I've got it! I've got it!' he whinnied in delight.

Willow sighed. It was great that Troy knew Arcadia so well because it meant they didn't have to spend ages studying the map. But by using his knowledge to race on ahead, Troy was taking the fun out of the treasure hunt for the rest of them.

'It would have been more fun if we'd all looked for the crystal together,' said Sapphire.

'Don't be silly. We have to find them as quickly as possible,' said Troy. 'That's the point.'

'Well, actually . . .' Willow began to argue. But before she could say any more, Troy was shushing her.

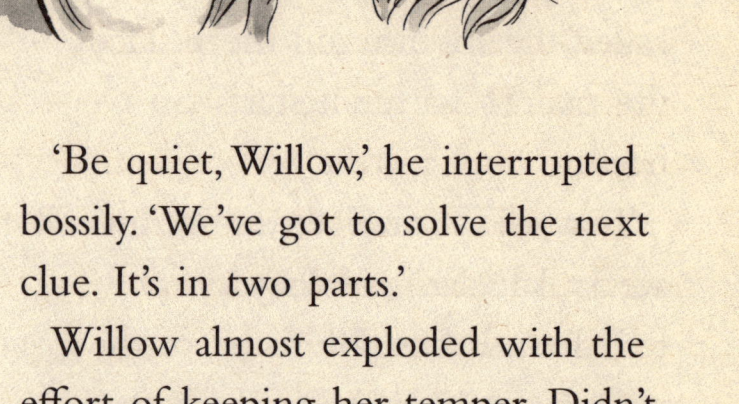

'Be quiet, Willow,' he interrupted
bossily. 'We've got to solve the next
clue. It's in two parts.'

Willow almost exploded with the
effort of keeping her temper. Didn't
Troy realize how annoying he was
being? Troy read the clue out. '"*I can
run but never walk. I have a mouth but
never talk. I have a bed but never sleep.
I have a head but never weep.*"' That's

the first part and the second says, "*A quiet noise is in my name. Find me quick and play the game!*"'

'The first part's easy,' said Storm. 'It's talking about a river. Water runs in a river and the end of the river is called the mouth and the head of the river is where it starts. So we need to find a river.'

'But which one? There are lots all across Arcadia,' said Troy.

'It sounds like the name of the river has something to do with a quiet noise,' said Willow. 'Let's look at the map.' She picked it up with her mouth.

'Here, let me look!' said Troy, trying to take it from her.

'No, I want to see,' said Willow, holding on tight.

'Let me look!' repeated Troy.

'No!' Willow exclaimed. Her voice was muffled by the map in her mouth and she was feeling crosser and crosser with Troy. 'We're supposed to be a team, Troy! You can't do everything on your own. It's not fair! Let *me* look this time!'

'No!' Troy yanked at it with his teeth. There was a loud ripping sound.

Willow and Troy stared at each other. They each had half the map in their mouths. It had torn in two!

Chapter Six

The Noise in the Trees

'Oh no!' Storm exclaimed.

'It wasn't me!' both Willow and Troy said immediately.

'It *was* you!' Willow whinnied furiously at Troy. 'You should have let me see!'

'You shouldn't have tried to hang

on to it!' said Troy. 'You're the one who ripped it!'

'No, I didn't!'

'Stop arguing, you two!' Sapphire whinnied.

'Yes! It was both your faults,' said Storm. 'You shouldn't have been quarrelling over the map. Now it's ripped and we're not even going to be able to finish the treasure hunt let alone win it! Just look at it!'

The map had a big jagged tear down the centre.

'If we put the two halves back together we might be able to read it,' said Sapphire hopefully as Willow and Troy glared at each other. 'Let's try.'

They carefully placed the bits of map next to each other. It was hard to read the writing where the rip was but Willow could just make out some words that labelled a river on the map. 'The Whispering River,' she said.

'That must be where the next clue is!' said Sapphire. 'It's a river and whispering is a quiet noise!'

'Let's go!' said Troy.

They flew there side by side. Willow didn't say a word to Troy. She was feeling so cross with him; she knew that if she spoke they'd end up arguing and she didn't want to upset Sapphire and Storm. At last they reached the river. It glittered in the sunlight, stretching up towards the mountains in one direction and down to the sea in another. All around it the land was covered with snow. 'I wonder where the crystal is,' said Sapphire.

'Let's separate and each search a different bit,' Troy said. 'I'll go up to where it starts in the mountains. Sapphire, you search the next bit. Willow, you search around here and,

Storm, you search nearer the sea.'

They all nodded. It looked like this clue was going to be really tough to find!

Willow began to search along the riverbank. After a little way the river entered some trees whose branches were bending down, heavy with snow. Willow trotted between the trees, her eyes scanning the ground looking for a bright crystal with a message attached.

Suddenly she heard a noise. It was a snuffling, snorting kind of noise. She stopped. It was coming from a nearby cluster of oak trees. It sounded like a creature, but what kind of creature made a noise like that?

Willow hesitated but then curiosity got the better of her and she walked over to the oak trees. Peering round the first one, she gasped! There, sitting on the ground, was a green baby dragon! It had two wings folded on its back, golden scales on its tummy and big dark eyes with long eyelashes.

It heard Willow gasp and jumped.

For a moment the baby dragon and Willow stared at each other.

'H-hello,' Willow said uncertainly. She'd never met a dragon before. They were very rare and her parents had told her they usually lived up in the mountains.

'Hello.' The dragon had a husky voice. It sounded almost as though it had been crying. 'Who . . . who are you?'

'I'm Willow,' Willow replied. 'What's your name?'

'Littleclaw,' said the dragon.

'Are you OK?' Willow asked him, stepping closer. Littleclaw was shivering.

The baby dragon shook his head.

'I'm cold and lost,' he said. 'I've only just learnt to fly. My parents told me not to go too far but, when I started flying down the mountain, it was such fun that I kept going. I went on and on and then landed here and now I can't seem to fly any more.' He looked hopefully at Willow. 'Can you help me? My mum and dad have told me stories about how unicorns look after the other creatures in Arcadia. Can you help me get home?'

Willow stared at him. 'I'd love to but I'm not a grown-up unicorn. I'm still at school.' She looked at the shivering dragon. Her heart went out to him. 'But maybe I can help.

Let me get my friends. Wait here a minute!'

'OK,' said Littleclaw. 'But you will come back soon, won't you?'

'I promise!' said Willow.

Willow raced to find Storm, Sapphire and Troy. They were astonished to hear about the dragon. Ten minutes later they were all standing in the clearing, staring at Littleclaw.

'So you really can't find your way home?' Sapphire said.

'No. After I landed by the river I found I couldn't take off again,' Littleclaw told her anxiously. 'I don't know why.'

Troy turned impatiently to the others. 'We're wasting time. His parents will come looking for him and he'll be fine. We need to get on and find our next clue.'

'Troy!' Willow said, shocked. 'We can't just leave him!'

'But we'll lose the treasure hunt if we help him!' Troy protested.

'That doesn't matter,' Sapphire said hotly. 'We're supposed to be the Guardians of Arcadia, Troy. Littleclaw needs our help!'

'Sapphire and Willow are right,' agreed Storm. 'The treasure hunt doesn't matter.' He breathed softly on the little dragon to try and warm him up. 'Don't worry, we'll help you find your way back home.'

The dragon looked at him gratefully. 'Thank you.'

For a moment, Troy looked torn, but then a stubborn look crossed his face. He shook his head. 'Let's finish the treasure hunt, get back to school and then we can tell the teachers about Littleclaw. They can help him if his parents haven't found him by then.'

'Oh, please don't leave me,' Littleclaw said anxiously.

Willow looked at him. 'Don't worry, we won't.' She glared at Troy. 'You can carry on with the treasure hunt if you want, Troy. We're going to help Littleclaw.'

'Fine,' Troy said angrily. 'If you're going to be like that, I'll finish the treasure hunt on my own!'

And he turned and cantered out of the trees.

Chapter Seven

Lost!

'I can't believe Troy's gone!' said Willow.

'Me neither,' said Sapphire, looking shocked. 'I know winning the treasure hunt's important to him but I never thought he'd go off like that. Not when Littleclaw needs our help.'

'Let's try and forget about it for now,' said Storm. 'We need to concentrate on helping Littleclaw get home.' He looked at the baby dragon. 'Why can't you fly?'

'I don't know but whenever I try nothing happens,' replied Littleclaw.

'Have a go,' suggested Willow.

They all watched as Littleclaw stretched out his wings. 'OK.'

He blew hard and leapt upwards. He beat his green wings and his legs scrabbled in the air but he didn't fly upwards. He just flopped back to the ground and landed with a thump. 'See.'

Storm frowned thoughtfully. 'Let's think about this. You're doing

everything you normally do?'
Littleclaw nodded.

'I thought dragons had to let out
a puff of smoke before they flew,'
Sapphire said. 'That's what we were
told in our healing class.'

'We do,' said Littleclaw.

'But you didn't do that then,'
Willow told him.

'Didn't I?' Littleclaw looked

surprised. 'I thought I did. Look.' He blew out hard but not even a wisp of smoke left his nostrils. 'Oh,' he said in alarm.

'I bet it's because you've got too cold in the snow!' Storm exclaimed. 'Sirona told us about it in healing. She said that when dragons, particularly young ones, get really cold, their fire goes out. They need healing magic to get it working again.' He turned to Willow. 'You're easily the best out of all of us at healing, Willow. Why don't you have a go at healing Littleclaw.'

'Oh yes, please do! Please!' the little dragon said, bouncing up and down in excitement.

Willow took a deep breath. 'OK,' she said. 'But I've never done anything like this before.'

Sapphire looked at her. 'Just believe you can do it,' she said. 'You know that's what we're always being told is the most important thing when we do magic.'

Willow looked at Littleclaw. Sapphire was right. *I can do it*, she thought. *I can heal him.* Shutting her eyes she imagined a fire burning inside her. She felt her whole body tingle. She could feel the magic building and glowing. She opened her eyes and touched her horn to Littleclaw's chest. She saw her horn glow silver, heard the little dragon

gasp, felt magic spark through her and run into him.

'I feel all warm!' Littleclaw cried.

Willow lifted her horn. 'See if you can blow smoke now!'

Littleclaw breathed out in a whoosh. A puff of grey smoke shot out of his nostrils. 'My fire's back!' he cried. He puffed again, stretched his wings and then next minute he was rising off the ground. With one flap of his wings he soared upwards towards the branches. 'I can fly again! You've cured me, Willow!'

Willow, Sapphire and Storm exchanged delighted looks. The baby dragon flew around the oak tree. 'Whee!'

The unicorns all flew up to join him. Together they glided through the branches and into the sky. Littleclaw's wings beat hard.

'Now you can fly home,' Sapphire told the little dragon. 'Whereabouts do you live?'

Littleclaw looked round and an uncertain frown crossed his face. 'I . . . er . . . I don't know.'

'What do you mean, you don't know?' asked Willow.

'Well, I think it's called Dragon's Point or Dragon's Peak . . .' Littleclaw looked unsure. 'I *think* it's Dragon's Peak. I know it's in the mountains but I don't know which ones.'

They all looked around. There were mountains to the north, the east and the west.

'What are we going to do?' Willow asked the others.

'Maybe the map will help,' suggested Sapphire.

'Yes, good idea,' Willow agreed. 'You stay here, Littleclaw,' she said, not wanting the dragon to see they were feeling really worried. 'And we'll look at the map.' They landed and looked at the two halves of the map but, although the mountains were all marked, there was nothing to suggest which bit was called Dragon's Peak. Willow's heart sank. She looked at Sapphire and Storm. 'What are we going to do?'

Just then there was a soft cough behind them. They swung round. Troy was standing there.

'Troy!' Willow gasped.

Troy hung his head. 'I . . . I'm sorry,' he said. 'I shouldn't have gone off like that. I got to the next clue and I realized I don't want to do the treasure hunt on my own. And I do want to help Littleclaw.'

Sapphire trotted over and nuzzled him. 'Oh, Troy.'

'I wish I hadn't been so stupid,' he said.

Willow felt a rush of relief. It had been horrible to think of Troy going off without them. 'You came back,' she told him. 'That's all that matters. Oh, Troy, I'm so glad you did.'

'Me too,' he said. 'How's Littleclaw?'

'Flying again,' said Storm. 'He'd lost his puff but Willow healed him.'

'Cool!' Troy said, looking admiringly at Willow.

'The only problem is that now he can't remember his way home. He thinks he lives in a place called Dragon's Peak,' said Willow. 'But he doesn't know where it is or how to get there.'

Troy stamped a hoof. 'I do.'

'Really?' said Willow.

Troy nodded. 'Dragon's Peak was marked on several of the old treasure maps I learnt in the library. It's not marked on our map because none of our clues led us there, but I'm sure I can find it.'

'What are we waiting for, then?' Willow said in delight. 'Let's go!'

Dragon's Peak

Willow and her friends flew into the sky. Littleclaw was waiting for them, looking worried.

'It's all right, Littleclaw!' Willow called. 'Troy's come back and he thinks he knows how to get you home to Dragon's Peak.'

'It might be a good idea just to

check that's where you really do live and that your parents are there,' said Sapphire, 'rather than fly all the way there and find it's not the right place.'

'How can we do that?' said Littleclaw.

'Rose quartz,' said Sapphire. 'I can use it to look at any place in Arcadia I want. There's some in the trees.'

They all flew down and Sapphire touched her horn to the rose quartz she had seen. 'Dragon's Peak,' she murmured.

There was a purple flash and the rock glowed like a mirror. Smoke spread out over the surface. As it cleared, Willow could see a picture in the rock. It showed a mountain with a summit covered in a pink cloud. There was a cave in the mountainside and a large green dragon was standing outside the cave, calling out anxiously.

'That's my mum!' cried Littleclaw.

'So that is your home! You *do* live on Dragon's Peak,' said Sapphire.

'Let's go, then!' said Troy.

Sapphire took her horn away from the rock and the picture vanished. The unicorns and Littleclaw rose into the air. As they flew above the trees a few flakes of snow swirled down.

Littleclaw shivered as the snow fell

on his wings. 'I don't like flying in the snow. It's really cold!'

'Fly close to me,' Willow told the little dragon. 'We don't want to risk your fire going out again!' She thought warm thoughts and the next second purple stars were shooting out of her horn.

'Oh, wow!' Littleclaw gasped, looking up in wonder at the purple rainbow that arched over him and Willow, keeping the snow off them. 'You're so clever! All of you! I'm really glad you're here to look after me.'

Willow felt a glow of pride. It was lovely being able to help.

'Which way is it?' Sapphire called to Troy. They all had stars streaming out of their horns too.

'Dragon's Peak is on the mountains to the west,' he called. 'Follow me!'

The others joined him.

Willow grinned at Troy. 'You know, I never thought I'd say this, but I'm glad you wanted to win the treasure hunt so much. If you hadn't been so keen you wouldn't have studied the maps and we wouldn't have known which way to go now.'

Troy smiled. 'True, but I wish I hadn't been so silly earlier. I should have realized that helping Littleclaw was more important than winning.'

'What made you come back?' Willow asked him.

'Well, I found the next clue but it wasn't any fun and as I was flying to the next place, I suddenly realized that I really wanted to be with all of you. I'd rather be helping Littleclaw than be on my own even if it means not winning the treasure hunt.'

Willow nudged him happily with her nose. 'I'm so glad you came back!'

'Me too.' Troy snorted. 'Anyway, even if I had carried on, I wouldn't have won the treasure hunt. Storm's the one who's really good at solving clues. I'm rubbish at it.'

'We're all good at different things,' Sapphire said. 'You're great at finding your way to places, Troy. Storm's really good at working out puzzles. Willow, you're really good at healing, which helped Littleclaw get his puff back.' She frowned. 'I don't know what I'm good at.'

'Making sure we don't argue too much!' Willow said. 'And you're brilliant at rose-quartz gazing!'

'We make a great team when we work together,' said Troy.

'The best!' said Storm.

They all whinnied happily and galloped on through the snowy sky.

When they reached their destination, Troy led the way to a jagged mountain with stony outcroppings that looked like dragon's teeth. There was a pink cloud above it just like the picture in the rose quartz.

'This is Dragon's Peak,' said Troy.

'It is! It is!' cried Littleclaw,

blowing out a puff of s[...]
excitement.

The pink cloud cast a gl[...]
the whole mountain. It seem[...]
have a similar effect to the unicorns'
purple rainbows – keeping
everywhere warm. There wasn't a
speck of snow on the mountainside,
just green grass and a winding clear
stream.

Willow and the others let their
purple rainbows disappear as they
landed on the sloping sides of the
mountain.

'There's my cave!' cried Littleclaw.
He bounded towards the entrance,
his wings flapping. 'Mum! Dad!'

There was a snort of relief and the

green dragon they'd seen in
e rose quartz hurried to the cave
entrance. 'Littleclaw!' she exclaimed,
her dark eyes widening in delight.

Littleclaw charged over. 'Mum!'

The big dragon folded her wings
round him and hugged him tight.
'Oh, Littleclaw, where have you
been? We've been so worried about
you. Your father's out looking for
you.'

'I flew too far and then lost my
puff and couldn't fly.' Littleclaw
explained what had happened. His
mother looked gratefully at Willow
and the others.

'Thank you so much for bringing
Littleclaw home,' she said.

'That's OK!' said
Willow happily.
The dragon
lifted her head
and blew out
three short
smoke rings. They
floated into the
sky. 'Your father
will see the smoke
and realize you're
back,' she said
to Littleclaw.

He snuggled against her. 'I'm sorry
I got lost, Mum.'

Willow glanced at her friends.
They were all smiling. It felt
wonderful to have brought

Littleclaw back safely. 'We should go back to school now,' said Willow.

'You must take something with you,' said Littleclaw's mother. 'To say thank you for finding Littleclaw. Here!' She turned her head and plucked a scale gently from her tail. It glinted and glimmered like an emerald as she held it out to them. It was beautiful. The unicorns stared at it in awe. None of them had ever seen a dragon's scale before.

'Thank you.' Troy bowed and took it. He put it into the leather bag and then set off into the sky. 'Bye, Littleclaw!'

'Bye!' Littleclaw called. 'Thank you for helping me.'

He and his mum watched them go. As the unicorns flew away from the Dragon's Peak they saw another big green dragon heading swiftly towards the cave.

'I bet that's Littleclaw's dad,' said Willow in delight. 'I'm so glad we helped him!'

'Me too!' said Sapphire. 'Even if it has meant we've lost the treasure hunt.'

Storm and Troy both whinnied in agreement.

'At least now we can just have fun finding the rest of our objects,' said Willow. She shot forward. 'Come on! We've still got three left to find!'

Chapter Nine

Wish Magic

Willow, Storm, Sapphire and Troy raced through Arcadia, finding their three remaining objects: a red crystal in an old tree trunk in Wilderness Wood, a yellow crystal hidden under a mossy bank in Moonflower Vale and a pink crystal hidden in a sparkling rock pool on Mermaid Beach.

'We've got them all,' Willow said in delight as Troy put the last crystal into the bag. 'Now we can go back to school!'

As they flew back they joined a crowd of other unicorns also flying back to school, their bags bulging with crystals.

'I wonder which team won,' said Sapphire as they flew through the school gates.

They flew over to the platform where a group of unicorns was standing round the teachers and the Tricorn. 'Who won?' Willow called out.

Oriel, a Year Three unicorn, looked up and whinnied. 'My team did! We got back here ages ago. We're going to have all the shamrock!'

'Well done!' Troy said sportingly. He put down their bag on the table.

Atlas emptied it out. As the dragon scale slid on to the tabletop, everyone gasped. 'What's this?' Atlas exclaimed. He picked it up. It glinted and shone in the light.

'It's a dragon's scale.' The Tricorn's deep voice broke the silence. He walked over and looked at the scale. 'How did you get this?' he asked curiously, looking at Willow, Storm, Troy and Sapphire.

'We helped a baby dragon,' Willow said. 'He was lost.' The story about Littleclaw poured out of her. All the other unicorns listened spellbound. 'We *had* to help him,' Willow said to the Tricorn as she finished, hoping they weren't in trouble. 'We couldn't have left him.'

The Tricorn smiled. 'No, you did just the right thing. You all acted as true future Guardians of Arcadia.' Willow felt a rush of relief and pride. 'And now you are lucky enough to have this.'

The Tricorn held up the scale.

'It's beautiful, isn't it,' said Sapphire happily.

'It's more than just beautiful, Sapphire,' the Tricorn told her seriously. 'Dragons' scales are immensely valuable. They are full of wish magic.'

'So, we can use it to wish for something?' Storm said.

'Yes,' the Tricorn told him. 'You should be very honoured the mother dragon gave you such a gift. But use it well. Each scale will only grant a single wish.'

Willow looked round at her friends. 'What are we going to wish for?'

'We should decide together,' said Troy. 'As a team.'

'We'll have to think about it very carefully,' said Sapphire.

Storm nodded.

'Go and think about it,' the Tricorn told them.

Storm took the scale and he and the others walked a bit away from the platform. 'What should we wish for?' Storm said, putting the scale down on the snow.

'I don't know,' said Willow.

'New bags for us all?' said Sapphire.

'New stable blankets?' suggested Troy.

'A feast,' said Storm.

'How about some shamrock, seeing as we didn't win the treasure hunt?' Willow suggested.

They looked at each other.

'All those wishes would be good but they don't seem somehow special enough,' said Sapphire slowly.

Willow knew exactly what Sapphire meant.

Just then there was the sound of disappointed whinnies behind them. They swung round. Oriel and his team were standing by the wooden crates of shamrock.

'The shamrock's ruined!' Willow heard Oriel exclaim. She wondered what he meant.

Atlas trotted over with Sirona. 'The lids on the crates weren't done up tightly enough,' he said. 'Shamrock goes off in the cold weather and it's been out here all day with the frost getting to it.'

Oriel and his friends looked really upset.

'Don't worry,' Atlas told them. 'You might not be able to have a term's supply of shamrock for winning but we'll find you another prize. A trophy or a medal or something.'

Oriel bit his lip. 'OK,' he said slowly.

Willow felt very sorry for him and

his friends. A trophy or a medal was nice but nowhere near as amazing as a term's supply of shamrock. An idea exploded into her brain. She swung round quickly to the others. 'I've got it! I know what we can wish for!'

'What?' Troy asked.

Willow beamed. 'A term's supply of shamrock – *for the whole school*!'

The others gasped.

'That's a brilliant idea!' whinnied Storm.

'Just perfect!' said Sapphire.

'Come on, let's tell the Tricorn!' Troy exclaimed.

Ten minutes later, all the unicorns – teachers and students – were standing round the wooden table munching delightedly on great piles of delicious shamrock.

Willow sighed in contentment. There were lots more crates of shamrock kept safely in one of the feed stores. Enough shamrock for everyone to have some every day for the rest of the term. The Tricorn had been delighted by their wish.

'I can see the dragons made a wise choice when they gave you a wishing scale,' he said. 'I'm very proud of you all.'

The words echoed round in Willow's head. She felt as if she was glowing. She and her friends might not have won the treasure hunt that day but it didn't matter. They'd had a great adventure, helped Littleclaw and they'd made everyone in the school really happy. What could be better?

Troy nudged her. 'It's been a good day, hasn't it?'

'It's been fantastic!' Willow looked at him and smiled.